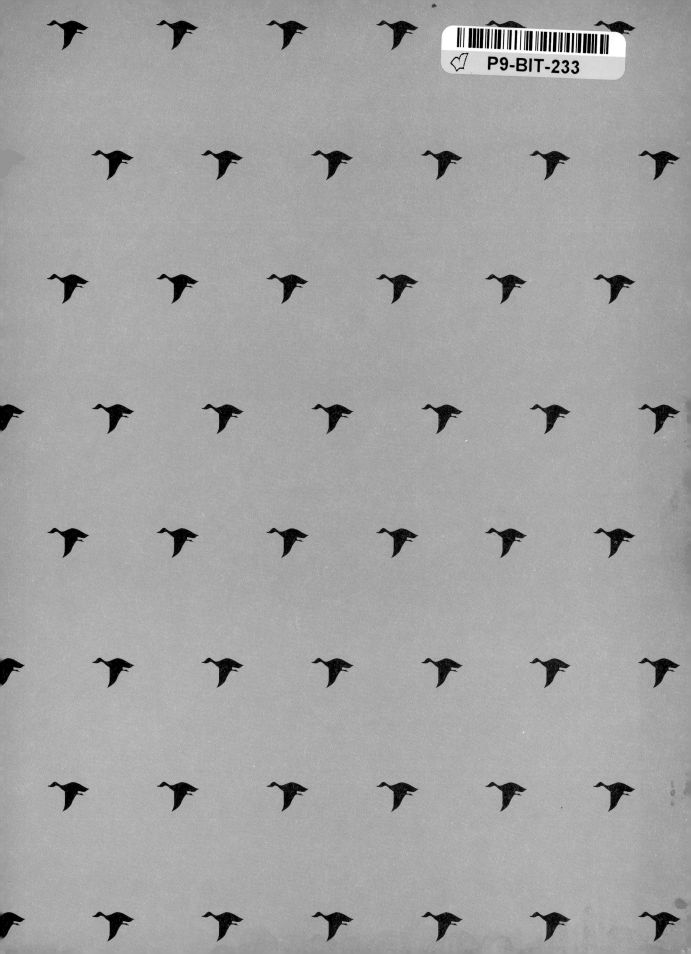

AESOP'S FABLES

Illustrated by
Walt Sturrock

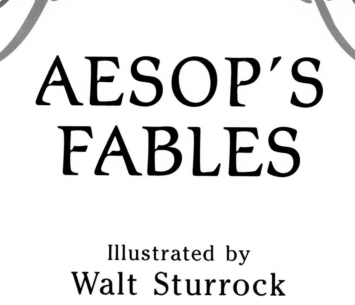

The Unicorn Publishing House
New Jersey

THE HARE AND THE TORTOISE

T he Hare, laughing, one day at the Tortoise for his slowness and general unwieldiness, was challenged by the latter to run a race. The Hare, thinking this would be great fun, and a greater joke by far, consented. The Fox was selected to act as umpire and hold the stakes. The race began, and the Hare, of course, soon left the Tortoise far behind. Having come midway to the end, she began to play about, nibbling on the young grass, and amusing herself in many ways. The day was quite warm, so she thought she would take a little nap in a soft, shady spot. If by chance the Tortoise should pass her while she slept, she knew she could easily overtake him again before he reached the end. The Tortoise, meanwhile, plodded on, unwavering and unresting, straight toward his goal. The Hare, having overslept, started up from her nap, and was surprised to find that the Tortoise was nowhere in sight. Off she went at full speed, but on reaching the finish line she found that the Tortoise was already there, waiting for her arrival.

Slow and steady wins the race.

THE SHIPWRECKED IMPOSTOR

The shipwrecked Chimp had been clinging for some time to a small board, when a Dolphin came up and offered to carry him ashore. This kind offer was immediately accepted, and, as they moved along, the Chimp began to tell the Dolphin many marvelous tales, which were really nothing but a pack of lies.

"Well, well, you are indeed an educated fellow," said the Dolphin in admiration. "My schooling has been sadly neglected, as I went to sea when but a week old." Just then they entered a large bay, and the Dolphin, referring to it, said, "I suppose you know Herring Roads?" The Chimp, taking this for the name of a fellow, and not wishing to appear ignorant, replied: "Do I know Rhodes? Well, I should almost think so! He's an old college chum of mine, and related to our family by—" This was too much for the Dolphin, who immediately made a great leap, and then diving quickly down, left the impostor in the air for an instant before he splashed back and disappeared.

A liar deceives no one but himself.

THE CROW AND THE PITCHER

A Crow, half-dead with thirst, came upon a Pitcher which had once been full of water. But when the Crow put his beak into the mouth of the Pitcher, he found that very little water was left in it, and that he could not reach far enough down to get at it. He tried and he tried, but at last had to give up in despair. Then a thought came to him, and he took a pebble and dropped it into the Pitcher. Then he took another pebble and dropped it into the Pitcher. Then another, and another, and another, and another, and another, and still another, until at last he saw the water rise to the top. He was then able to drink deep of the water and save his life.

Necessity is the mother of invention.

THE NORTH WIND AND THE SUN

A dispute arose between the North Wind and the Sun, each claiming that he was stronger than the other. At last they agreed that each would try his power upon a traveler to see which could strip him of his cloak. The North Wind had the first try. Gathering up all his force for the attack, he came whirling furiously down upon the man, and caught up the cloak as though he would tear it from the man by one single effort: but the harder he blew, the more closely the man wrapped it around himself.

Then came the turn of the Sun. At first he beamed gently upon the traveler, who soon unclasped his cloak and walked along with it hanging loosely about his shoulders. The Sun then shone forth in his full strength, and the man, before he had gone but a few steps, was glad to throw his cloak right off and complete his journey more lightly clad.

Persuasion is better than force.

THE ANT AND THE GRASSHOPPER

On a field one summer's day a Grasshopper was hopping about, chirping and singing to its heart's content. An Ant passed by, carrying a great kernel of corn back to its nest.

"Why not come and chat with me," said the Grasshopper, "instead of working so hard?"

"I am helping to gather food for the winter," said the Ant, "and I suggest you do the same."

"Pooh! Why bother about winter?" said the Grasshopper; "we have plenty of food at present." But the Ant went on his way and continued to work. When the harsh winter came, the Grasshopper had no food and found himself dying of hunger, while he saw the ants ate corn and grain every day from the stores they had collected all summer long. Then the Grasshopper knew:

It is best to prepare
for the days of necessity.

THE ROSE AND THE AMARANTH

A Rose and an Amaranth blossomed side by side in a garden, and the Amaranth said to her neighbor, "How I envy you your beauty and your sweet scent! No wonder you are everyone's favorite."

But the Rose replied with a shade of sadness in her voice, "Ah, my dear friend, I bloom but for a short time: my petals will soon wither and fall, and then I must die. But your flowers never fade, even when they are cut; for they are everlasting."

Greatness bears its own burdens.

THE TOWN MOUSE AND THE COUNTRY MOUSE

Now there was once a Town Mouse who went to visit his cousin in the country. His cousin gave him a hearty welcome. Beans and bacon, cheese and bread, were all he had to offer, but he offered them freely. The Town Mouse rather turned up his long nose at this country fare, and said, "I can't understand, Cousin, how you can put up with such poor food as this, but, of course, you cannot expect anything better in the country. Come with me and I will show you how to live. When you have been in town a week, you will wonder how you could ever have stood a country life." No sooner said than done: the two mice set off for town and arrived late that night. "You will want some refreshment after our long journey," said the Town Mouse, and took his friend into a grand dining room. There they found the remains of a fine feast, and soon the two mice were eating up jellies and cakes and all that was nice. Suddenly, they heard growling and barking. "What is that?" said the Country Mouse. "It is only the dogs of the house," answered the other. "Only!" said the Country Mouse. "I do not like that music at my dinner!" Just at that moment in came two huge dogs, and the two mice had to run for their lives. "Good-bye, Cousin," said the Country Mouse. "What! Going so soon?" said the other. "Yes," he replied:

Better beans and bacon in peace,
than cakes and ale in fear.

THE VAIN JACKDAW

Jupiter announced that he would appoint a king over all the birds, and named a day on which they were to appear before his throne, when he would select the most beautiful of them all to be their ruler. Wishing to look their best for the occasion, they repaired to the banks of a stream, where they busied themselves in washing and preening their feathers. The Jackdaw was there along with the rest, and realized that, with his ugly feathers, he would have no chance of being chosen. So he waited until they were all gone, and then picked up the most gaudy of the feathers they had dropped, and fastened them about his own body. The result was that he looked gayer than any of them. When the appointed day came, the birds came before Jupiter. After passing in review, Jupiter thought the Jackdaw was by far the most beautiful. But just as he was about to proclaim the Jackdaw king, all the other birds gathered around the faker, and stripped him of the stolen feathers, exposing him for the fraud that he was.

It is not only fine feathers
that make fine birds.

THE DOVE AND
THE ANT

An Ant, going to a river to drink, fell in, and was carried along in the stream. A Dove took pity on her, and threw into the river a small bough, by means of which the Ant reached the shore. The Ant afterward, seeing a man pointing a gun at the Dove, stung him in the foot sharply, and made him miss his aim, and so saved the Dove's life.

Little friends may prove great friends.

THE LOST WIG

A funny old lion, who had the misfortune to lose his mane, was wearing a wig as he was taking a stroll on a very windy day.

Looking up, he saw one of the charming Tiger sisters across the street, and, wishing to make an impression, politely smiled and made a beautiful low bow. At that moment a very smart gust of wind came up, with the unhappy result being that his wig flew off and left him there, feeling foolish and looking worse, with his bald head glistening like a billiard ball. Though somewhat embarrassed at first, he smiled at the Lady and said: "Is it a wonder that another fellow's hair shouldn't keep on my head, when my own wouldn't stay there?"

Wit always has an answer ready.

THE CAGED BIRD
AND THE BAT

A singing bird was confined in a cage which hung outside a window, and had a way of singing at night when all other birds were asleep. One night a Bat came and clung to the bars of the cage, and asked the Bird why she was silent by day and sang only at night. "I have a very good reason for doing so," said the Bird. "It was once when I was singing in the daytime that a hunter heard my voice, and set his nets for me and caught me. Since then I have never sung except by night." But the Bat replied, "It is no use your doing that now when you are a prisoner: if only you had done so before you were caught, you might still be free."

Precautions are useless after the crisis.

THE DOG AND THE SHADOW

It happened that a Dog had got a piece of meat and was carrying it home in his mouth to eat it in peace. Now on his way home he had to cross a plank lying across a running brook. As he crossed, he looked down and saw his own shadow reflected in the water beneath. Thinking it was another dog with another piece of meat, he made up his mind to have that also. So he made a snap at the shadow in the water, but as he opened his mouth the piece of meat fell out, dropped into the water and was never seen again.

Beware of losing the substance
by grasping at the shadow.

THE TWO CRABS

One fine day two Crabs came out from their home to take a stroll on the sand. "Child," said the mother, "you are walking very ungracefully. You should accustom yourself to walking straight forward without twisting so from side to side."

"Pray, mother," said the child, "do but set the example yourself, and I will gladly follow you."

Example is the best guidance.

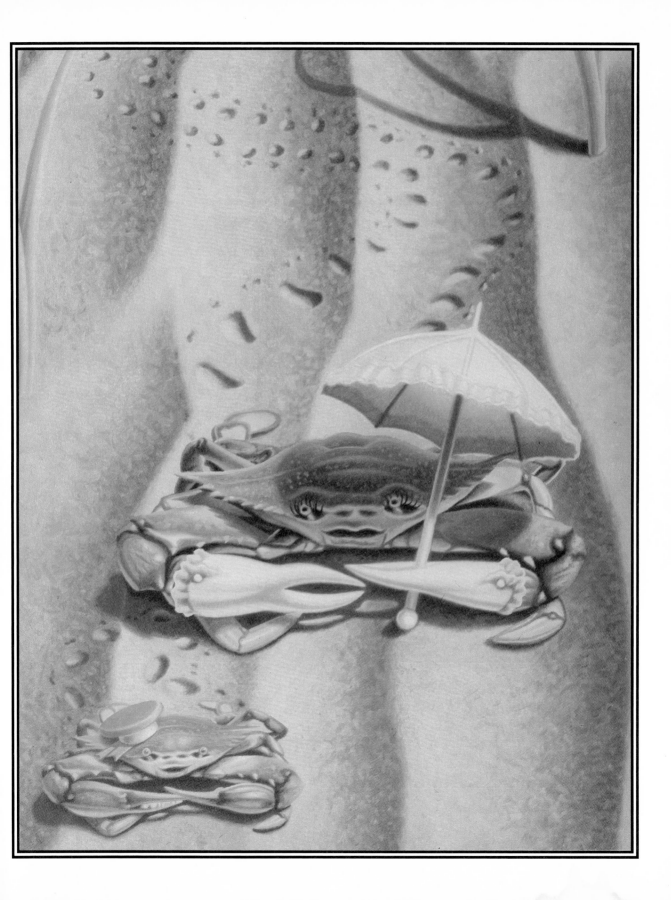

THE MILKMAID
AND HER PAIL

A farmer's daughter had been out to milk the cows, and was returning to the dairy carrying her pail of milk upon her head. As she walked along, she fell to musing after this fashion: "The milk in this pail will provide me with cream, which I will make into butter and take to market to sell. With the money I will buy a number of eggs, and when they hatch I shall have quite a large poultry yard. Then I shall sell some of my chickens, and with the money which they will bring in I will buy myself a new gown, which I shall wear when I go to the fair. All the young fellows will admire it, and come and ask to kiss me, but I shall toss my head and have nothing to say to them." Forgetting all about the pail, she tossed her head back as she spoke. Down went the pail, all the milk was spilled, and all her fine castles in the air vanished in a moment!

*Do not count your chickens
before they are hatched.*

THE FOX AND THE MASK

A fox had by some means got into the storeroom of a theatre. Suddenly he spotted a face glaring down on him, and began to be very frightened; but looking more closely he found it was only a Mask, such as actors use to put over their face. "Ah," said the Fox, "you look very fine; it is a pity you have not got any brains."

Outside show is a poor substitute
for inner worth.

LITTLE BOY
AND FORTUNE

A little boy wearied with a long journey, lay down on the very brink of a deep well. Being within an inch of falling into the water, Lady Fortune, it is said, appeared to him, and waking him from his slumber, told him: "Little boy, pray wake up: for had you fallen into the well, the blame would be thrown on me, and I would get an ill name among men; for I find that men are sure to blame their troubles on me, however much by their own folly they have really brought them on themselves."

Everyone is more or less master
of his own fate.

THE ANT AND
THE CHRYSALIS

An Ant nimbly running about in the sunshine in search of food came across a Chrysalis that was very near its time of change. The Chrysalis moved its tail, and thus attracted the attention of the Ant, who then saw for the first time that it was alive. "Poor, pitiable animal!" cried the Ant disdainfully. "What a sad fate is yours! While I can run hither and thither, at my pleasure, and, if I wish, climb the tallest tree, you lie imprisoned here in your shell, with power only to move a joint or two of your scaly tail." The Chrysalis heard all this, but did not try to make any reply.

A few days after, when the Ant passed that way again, nothing but the shell remained. Wondering what had become of the contents, he felt himself suddenly shaded and fanned by the gorgeous wings of a beautiful Butterfly. "Behold in me," said the Butterfly, "your much pitied friend! Boast now of your powers to run and climb as long as you can get me to listen." So saying, the Butterfly rose in the air, and, borne along and aloft on the summer breeze, was soon lost to the sight of the Ant forever.

Appearances can be deceptive.

THE BOY WHO CRIED WOLF

There was once a young Shepherd Boy who tended his sheep at the foot of a mountain near a dark forest. It was rather lonely for him all day, so he thought upon a plan by which he could get a little company and some excitement. He rushed down towards the village calling out, "Wolf, Wolf," and the villagers came out to meet him, and some of them stopped and spoke with him for some time. This pleased the boy so much that a few days afterwards he tried the same trick, and again the villagers came to his aid. But shortly after this a Wolf actually did come out from the forest, and began to worry the sheep, and the boy, of course, cried out "Wolf, Wolf," still louder than before. But this time the villagers, who had been fooled twice before, thought the boy was again deceiving them, and nobody stirred a foot to help him. So the Wolf made a good meal off the boy's flock, and when the boy began to complain, the wise man of the village said:

A liar will not be believed,
even when he speaks the truth.

THE FROGS AND
THE WELL

Two Frogs lived together in a marsh. But one hot summer the marsh dried up, and they left it to look for another place to live in: for frogs like damp places if they can get them. By and by they came to a deep well, and one of them looked down into it, and said to the other, "This looks a nice cool place. Let us jump in and settle here." But the other, who had a wiser head on his shoulders, replied, "Not so fast, my friend. Supposing this well dried up like the marsh, how should we then get out again?"

Look before you leap.

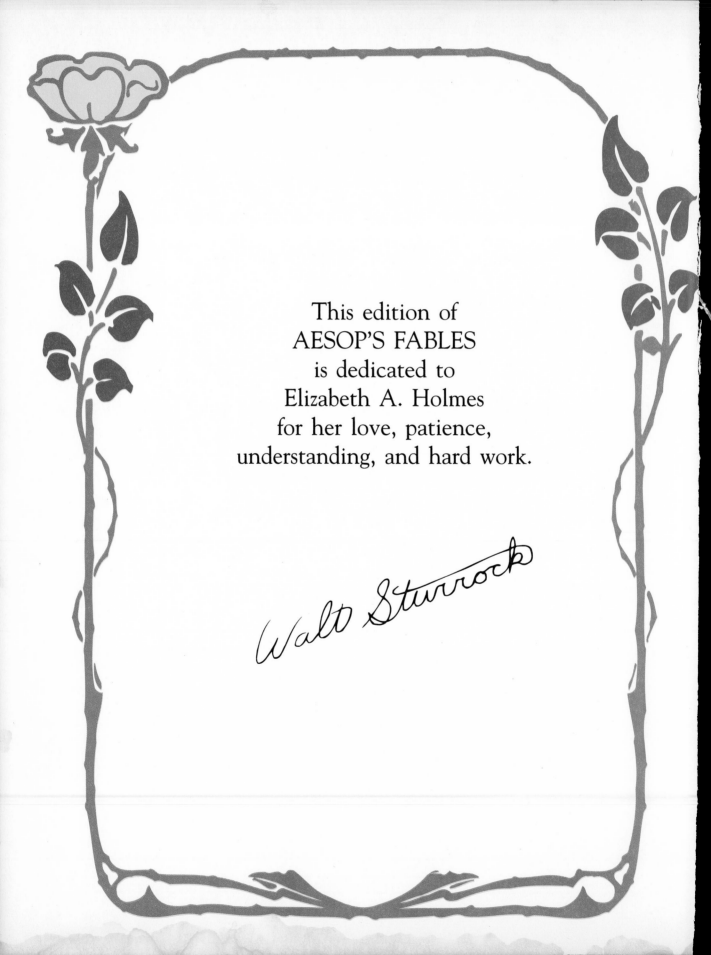

This edition of
AESOP'S FABLES
is dedicated to
Elizabeth A. Holmes
for her love, patience,
understanding, and hard work.

Walt Sturrock

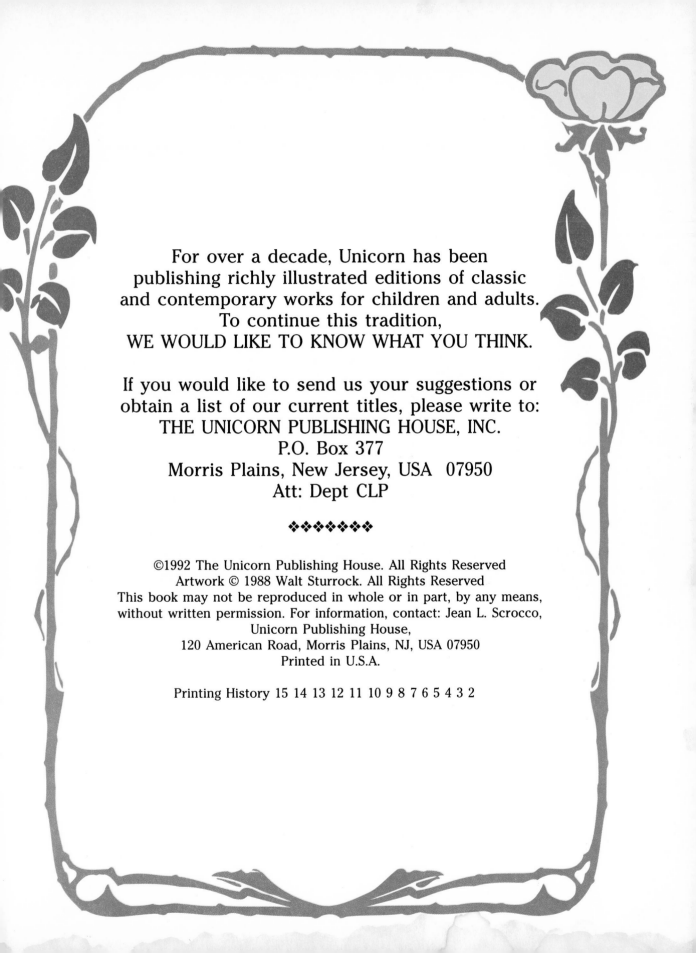

For over a decade, Unicorn has been
publishing richly illustrated editions of classic
and contemporary works for children and adults.
To continue this tradition,
WE WOULD LIKE TO KNOW WHAT YOU THINK.

If you would like to send us your suggestions or
obtain a list of our current titles, please write to:
THE UNICORN PUBLISHING HOUSE, INC.
P.O. Box 377
Morris Plains, New Jersey, USA 07950
Att: Dept CLP

❖❖❖❖❖❖❖

Printing History 15 14 13 12 11 10 9 8 7 6 5 4 3 2

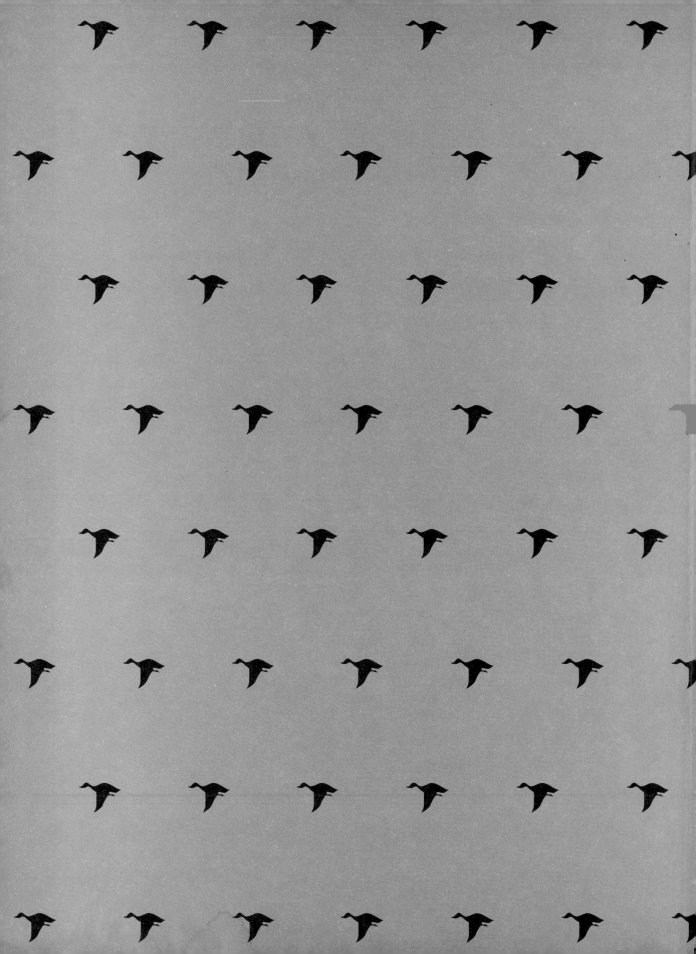